A Day With

GENIUS MINDS

A Day With

GENIUS MINDS

MOONSTONE

Published in Moonstone
by Rupa Publications India Pvt. Ltd 2023
7/16, Ansari Road, Daryaganj
New Delhi 110002

Sales centres:
Prayagraj Bengaluru Chennai
Hyderabad Jaipur Kathmandu
Kolkata Mumbai

P-ISBN: 978-93-5520-922-1
E-ISBN: 978-93-5520-923-8

First impression 2023

10 9 8 7 6 5 4 3 2 1

Printed in India

Contents

Stephen Hawking

Galileo Galilei

Albert Einstein

Isaac Newton

Stephen Hawking

Stephen Hawking discovered that black holes emit radiation.
Read on to know about his achievements.

Meet Tim and Tyra

Hi, I'm Tim.

Hi, I'm Tyra. We are going to visit Stephen Hawking. Let's meet him now.

Stephen William Hawking was born in Oxford, **England** on 8 January, 1942. He was a great **physicist** and **cosmologist**. He was one of the greatest **scientists** in the world.

Stephen Hawking suffered from a disease called **amyotrophic lateral sclerosis** (ALS). He was **diagnosed** with ALS when he was 21. But his disease did not stop him from studying and working hard. Stephen lost his speech after a **surgery** in 1985. He used a computer and a **speech synthesizer** to **communicate**.

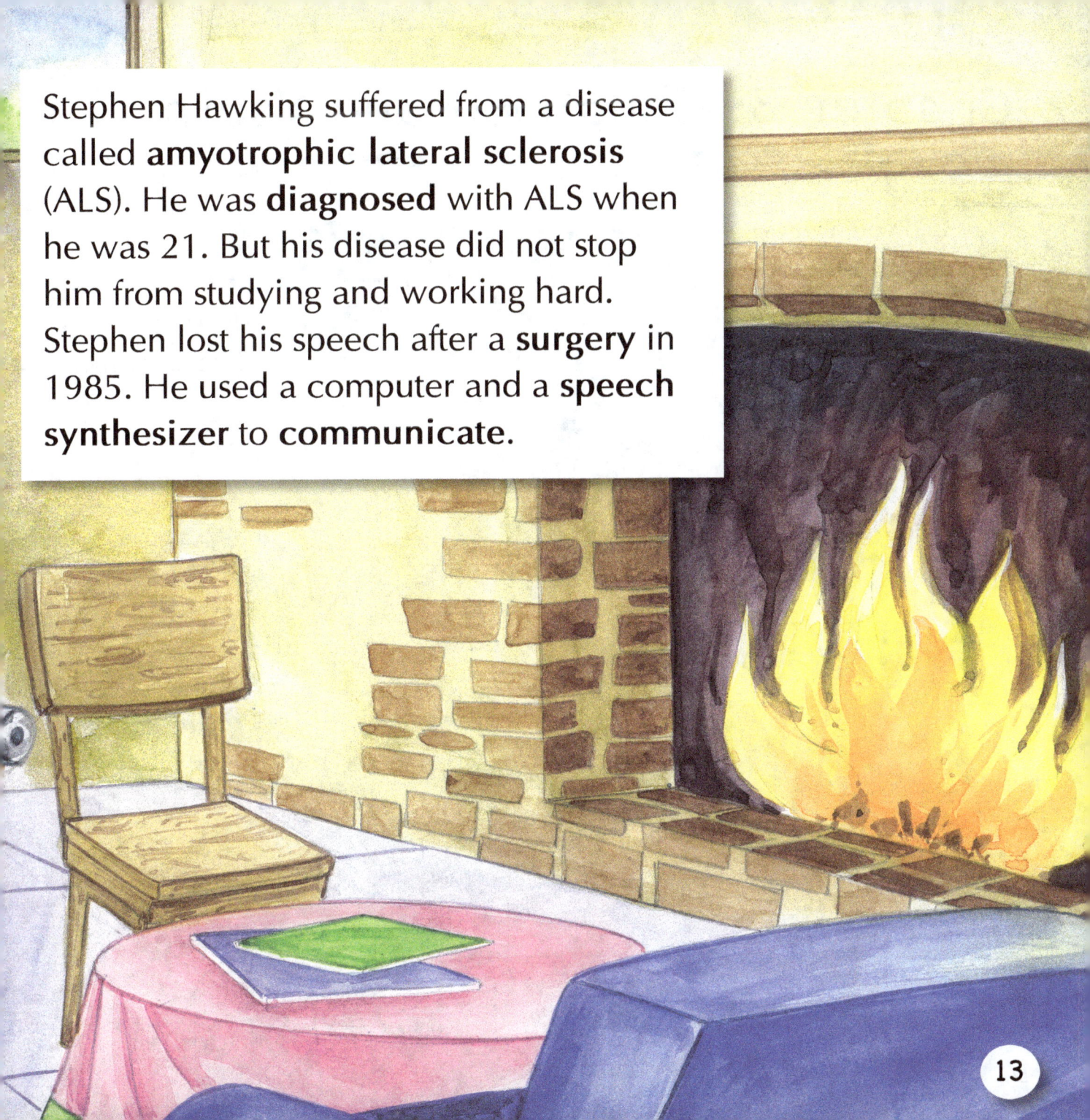

As a child, Stephen Hawking loved watching the sky and the stars. On summer evenings, he would stretch out in the backyard with his mother and siblings and watch the stars. Stephen joined University College at Oxford University at the age of 17. He wanted to study math. However, his college did not have any special courses in math. So, he studied physics and chemistry.

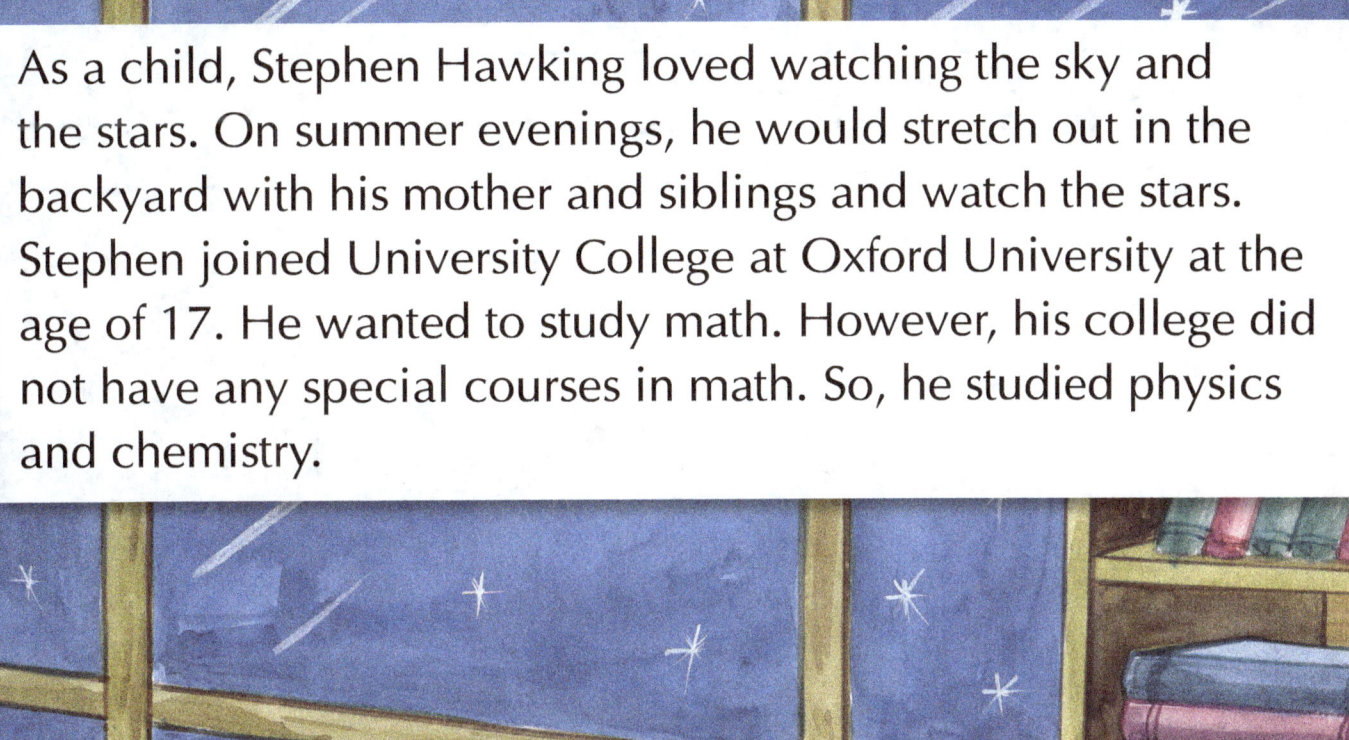

Chapter 4: Black Holes

Stephen Hawking spent many years studying black holes. He wrote many important papers on the subject. He discovered that **black holes** emit **radiation**. This radiation is now known as Hawking Radiation.

Chapter 5: A Brief History of Time

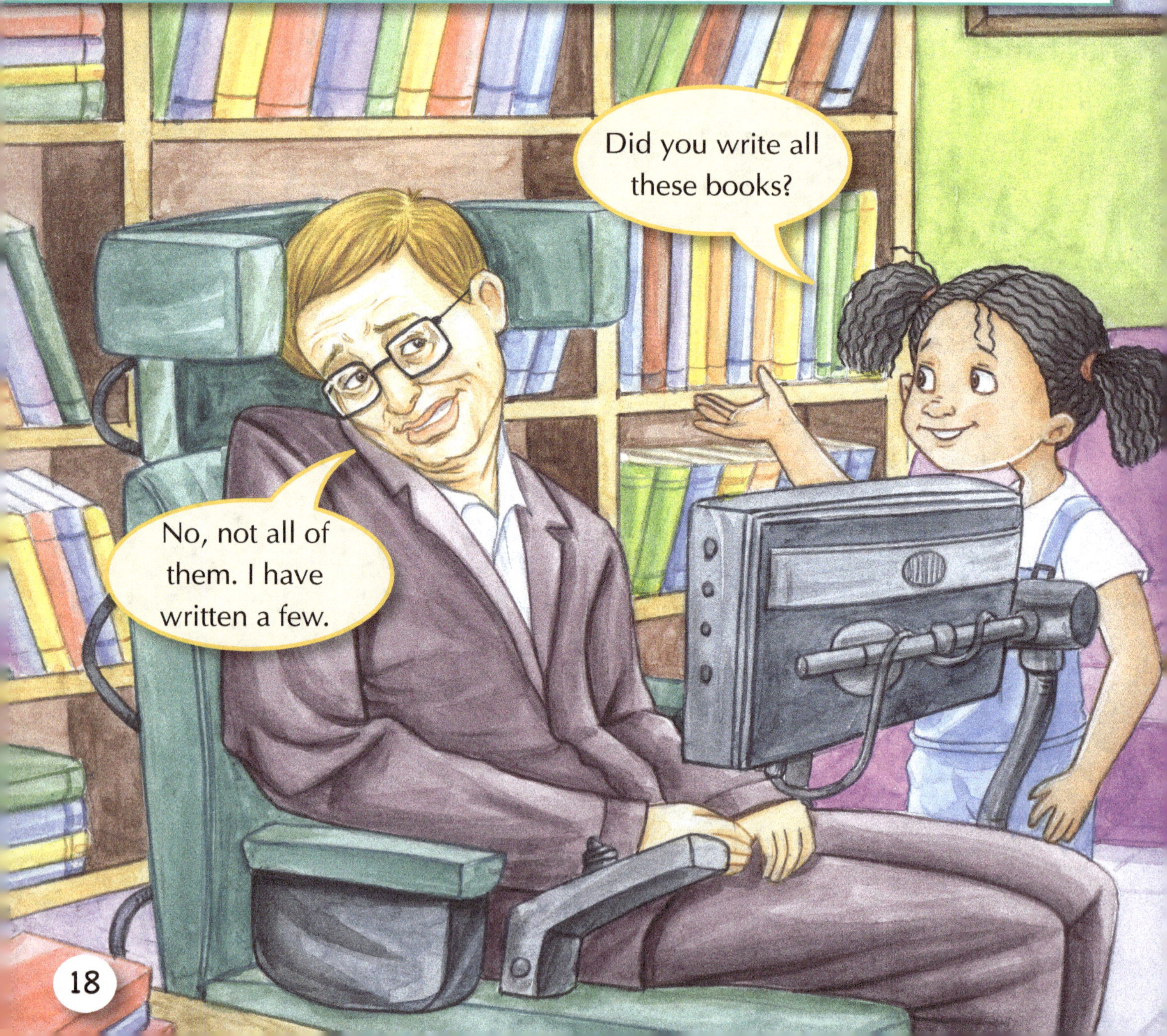

Stephen Hawking wanted everyone to understand about the universe. So, he wrote a book called *A Brief History of Time* in 1988. The book has sold more than 10 million copies around the world. In 2005, Hawking and Leonard Mlodinow, an American scientist, wrote a new book, *A Briefer History of Time*. This book has also sold millions of copies.

Stephen Hawking and Lucy wrote five books for children. The books are *George's Secret Key to the Universe*, *George's Cosmic Treasure Hunt*, *George and the Big Bang*, *George and the Unbreakable Code* and *George and the Blue Moon*.

Millions of children around the world have read these books.

Stephen Hawking worked at Cambridge University. In 1979, he became the Lucasian Professor of Mathematics at Cambridge. The Lucasian Chair of Mathematics is a very important position at Cambridge University.

Chapter 8: Awards and Recognitions

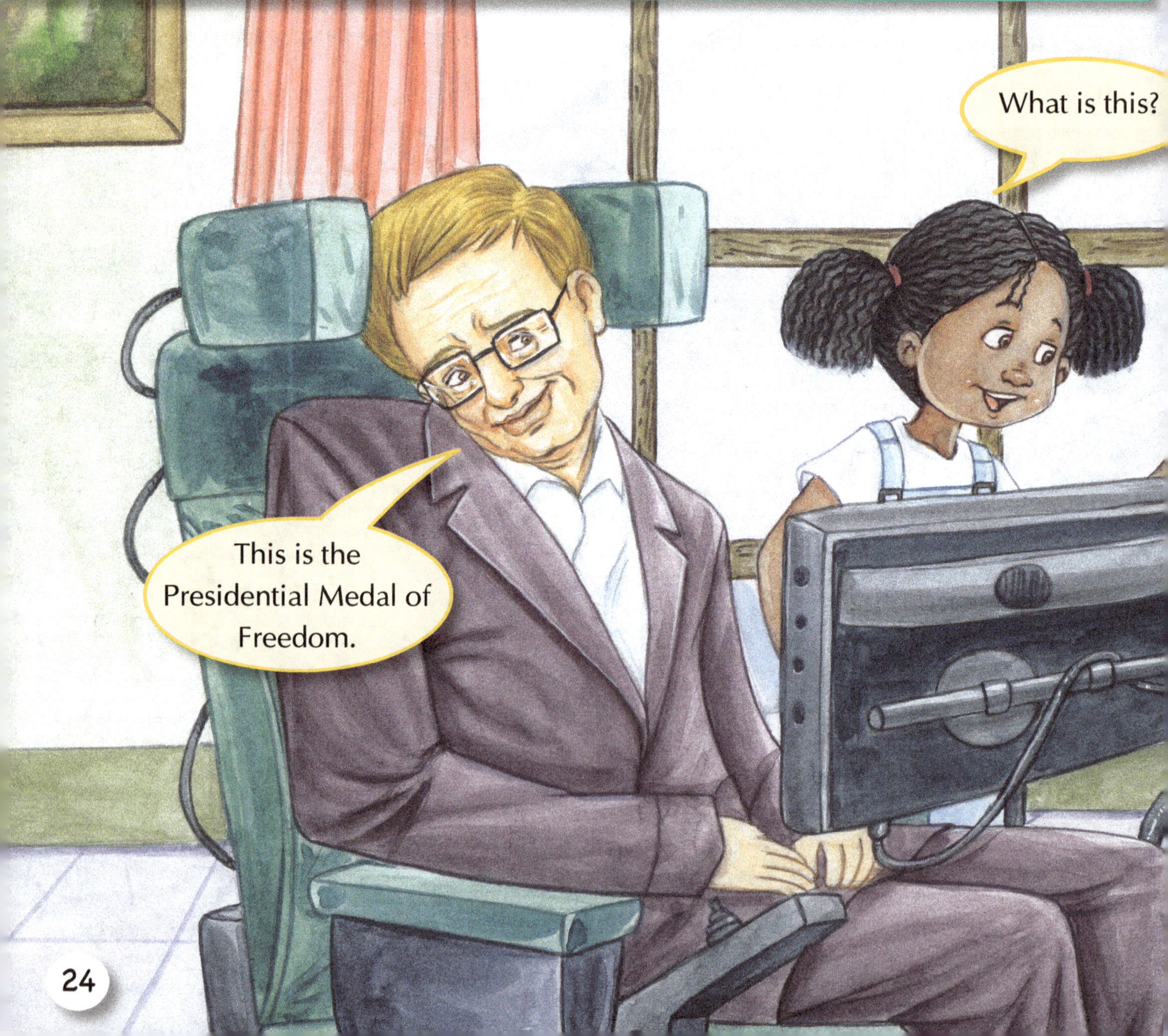

Stephen Hawking earned many awards for his great contributions to science.

He was awarded the Presidential Medal of Freedom in 2009 by the US President, Barack Obama. It is the highest civilian award in the **USA**.

In 2013, he was awarded the Russian Special Fundamental Physics Prize.

Stephen Hawking was one of the greatest physicist, cosmologist, astronomer and mathematician. His studies have helped us understand the universe better.

Hawking died on 14 March, 2018 in Cambridge, England.

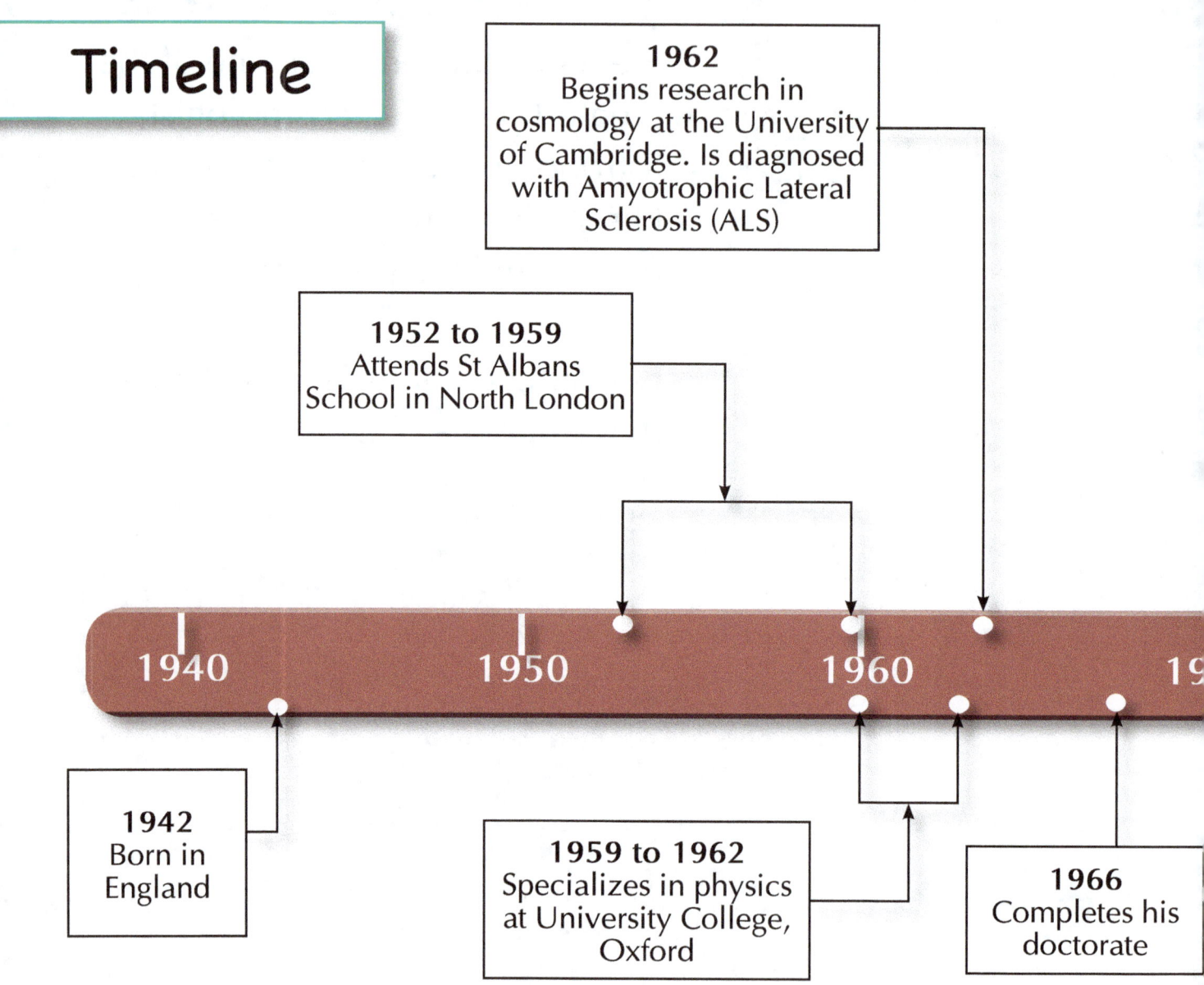

1962
Begins research in cosmology at the University of Cambridge. Is diagnosed with Amyotrophic Lateral Sclerosis (ALS)

1952 to 1959
Attends St Albans School in North London

1942
Born in England

1959 to 1962
Specializes in physics at University College, Oxford

1966
Completes his doctorate

1940   1950   1960   19

Stephen Hawking's Life and Work

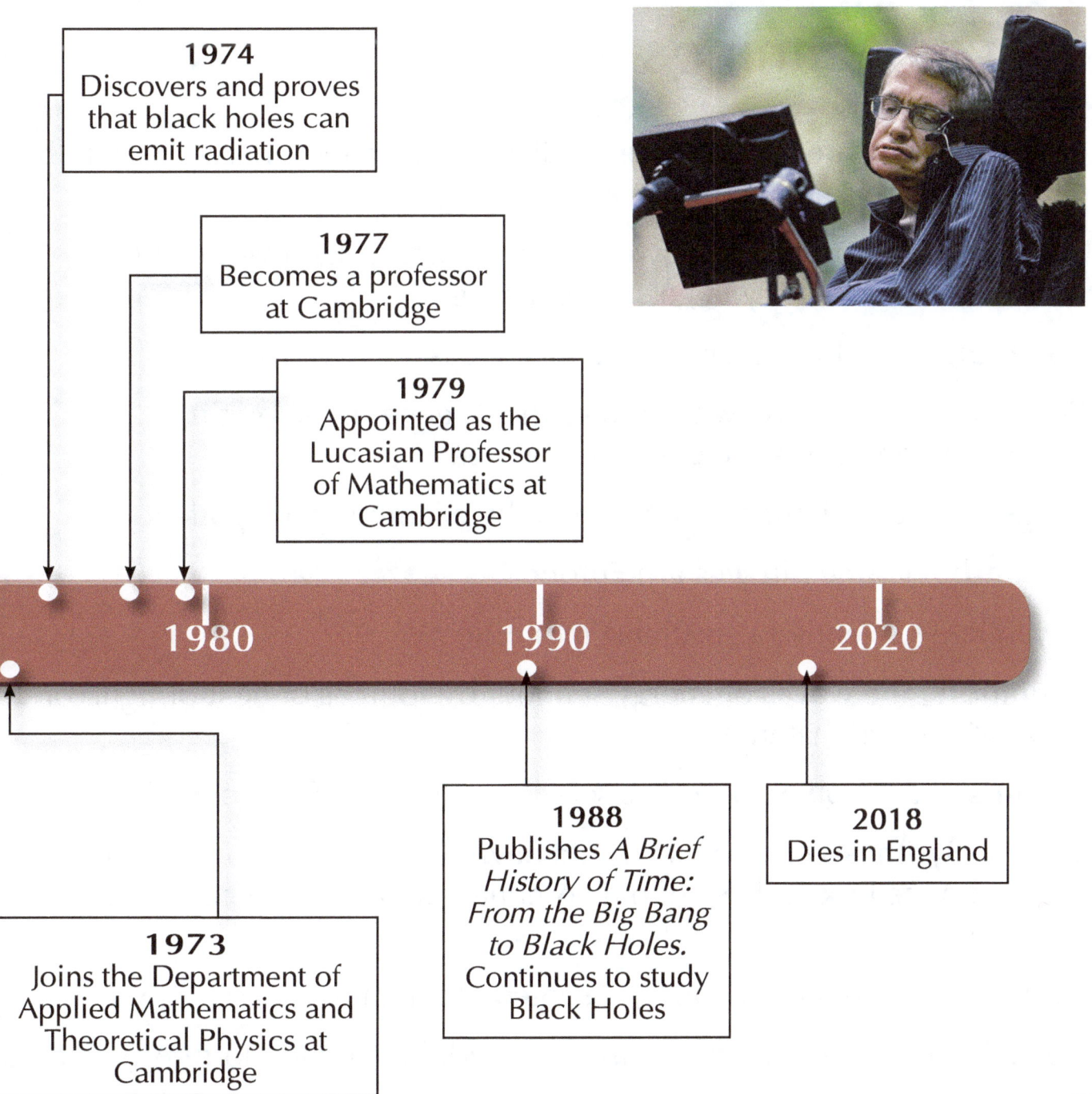

1974
Discovers and proves that black holes can emit radiation

1977
Becomes a professor at Cambridge

1979
Appointed as the Lucasian Professor of Mathematics at Cambridge

1980

1990

2020

1988
Publishes *A Brief History of Time: From the Big Bang to Black Holes.* Continues to study Black Holes

2018
Dies in England

1973
Joins the Department of Applied Mathematics and Theoretical Physics at Cambridge

Word Meanings

Amyotrophic Lateral Sclerosis: A disease that affects nerve cells in the brain and the spinal cord

Black Hole: A region or body in space. Scientists believe that black holes form when very large stars collapse

Communicate: To exchange thoughts, ideas, or information

Cosmologist: A person who studies the science of the origin, development, and structure of the universe

Diagnose: To find out about a disease by examining the patient

England: A country in western Europe

Physicist: A scientist, a specialist in physics

Radiation: The waves of energy sent out by sources of heat or light, or by radioactive material

Scientist: A person who studies science to learn and discover things

Speech Synthesizer: An electronic device that allows you to enter any text into the box and listen to a computer generated voice speaking the output

Surgery: An operation done by a surgeon to treat a disease

USA: The third largest country in the world, located in North America

Think, Talk and Write

Think About It

Stephen Hawking dicovered many things.
What do you think black holes look like?
Draw a picture of a black hole.

Talk About It

How would you describe Hawking?
Tell a friend about him.
Tell your friend what he did.

Write About It

Hawking made some great discoveries.
What would you like to discover?
Do you think there are people on other planets? Write three
sentences about it.

What did you learn from Stephen Hawking?

....

....

....

....

....

....

....

....

....

....

....

....

....

....

What are the five things that you will change after reading Stephen Hawking's story?

....
....
....
....
....
....
....
....
....
....
....
....
....
....

Galileo Galilei

Galileo Galilei is called the "father of science."
He figured out many things.
Read on to discover what he learned.

Meet Tim and Tyra

Hi, I'm Tim.

Hi, I'm Tyra. We are going to travel back in time to visit Galileo. Let's meet him now.

Galileo Galilei was born in Pisa, **Italy** on 15 February, 1564.

He was a scientist and an **inventor**.

He did many **experiments**.

He discovered many things.

People thought heavy objects fell faster.
Galileo Galilei was not sure.
He tested his idea. He went to a tall tower.
He dropped two balls at the same time.
One was heavy. One was light.
They both hit the ground at about the same time.
Heavy objects did not fall faster.

Galileo Galilei invented a **thermometer**.
It had a tube with water inside.
The water moved up when it was hot.
The water moved down when it was cold.

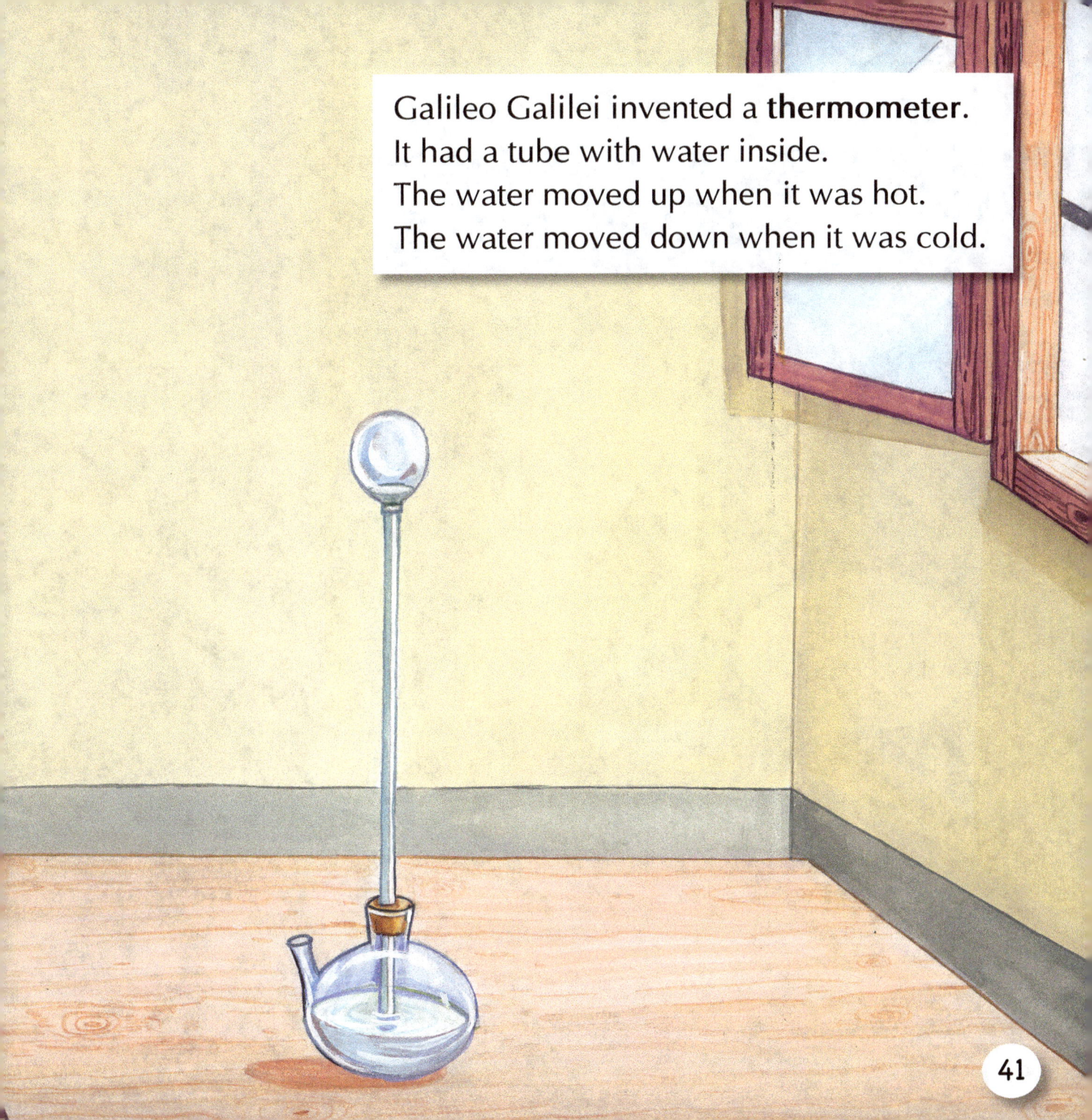

Chapter 4: The Telescope

Galileo Galilei was also an **astronomer**.
He wanted to look at the **planets** and stars.
They are far away. It is hard to see them.
So, Galileo made a **telescope**.
Then he could see them much better.

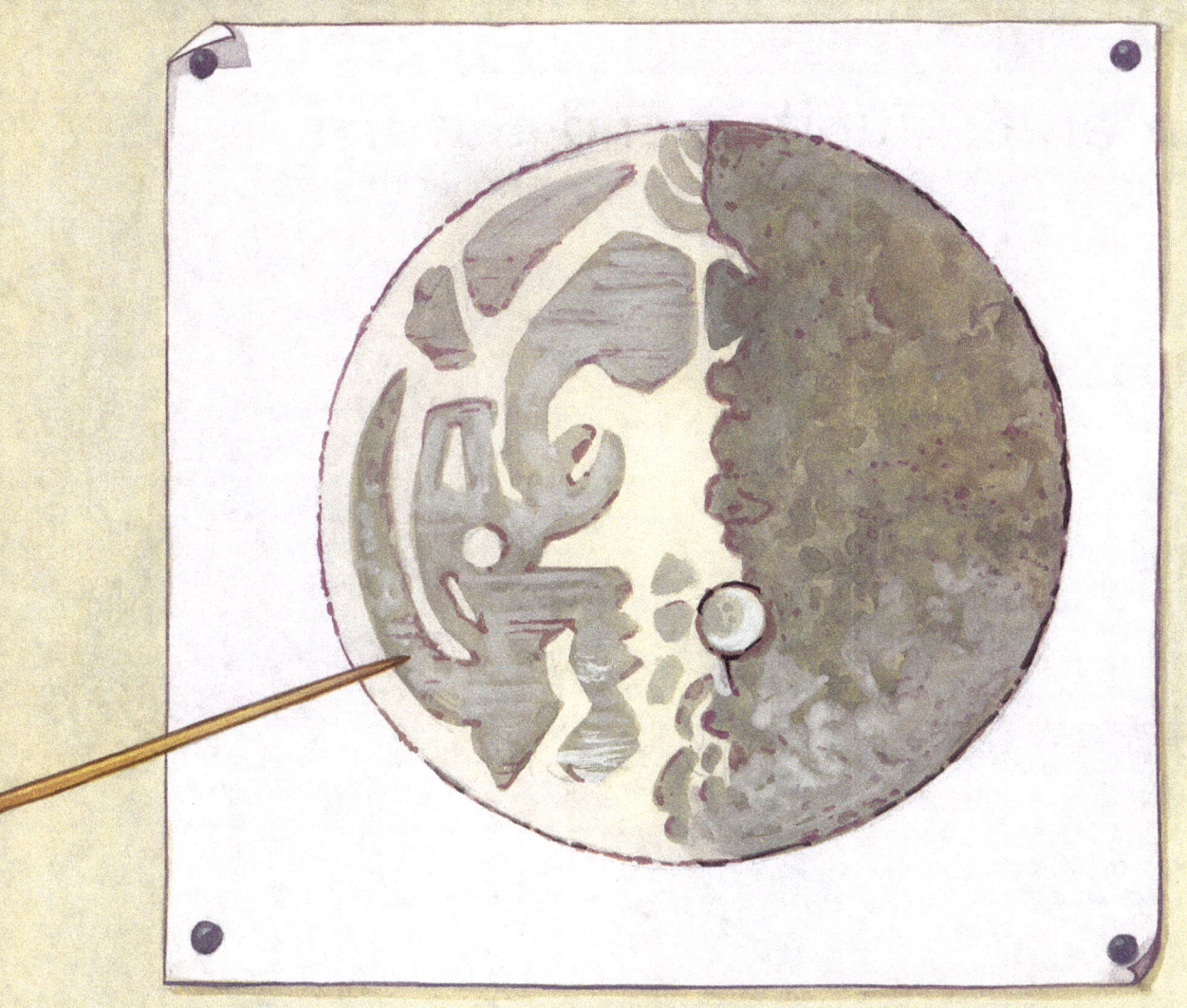

People thought the Moon was smooth and round.
Galileo Galilei used his telescope. He looked at the Moon.
It was not smooth. He could see mountains.
He could see valleys. He drew what he saw.

Galileo Galilei used his telescope to look at the planets.
He saw **Jupiter** and **Saturn**. He learned new things.
He saw four moons moving around Jupiter.
He saw rings of ice, dust and rocks around Saturn.

People thought the Sun and planets moved around the Earth.
Galileo Galilei used his telescope to look at the Sun and planets.
He saw the planets move around the Sun.
He discovered that the Earth is not the centre of the
Solar System.
The Sun is the centre!

Chapter 8: The Milky Way

Galileo Galilei studied our **galaxy**.
It looks like faraway clouds in the night sky.
He discovered that it consists of many stars.
It is called the **Milky Way**.

Galileo Galilei was a great scientist.
He had many new ideas. He proved them with experiments.
Therefore, he is called the "father of science."

Galileo died in Arcetri, Italy on 8 January, 1642.

Timeline

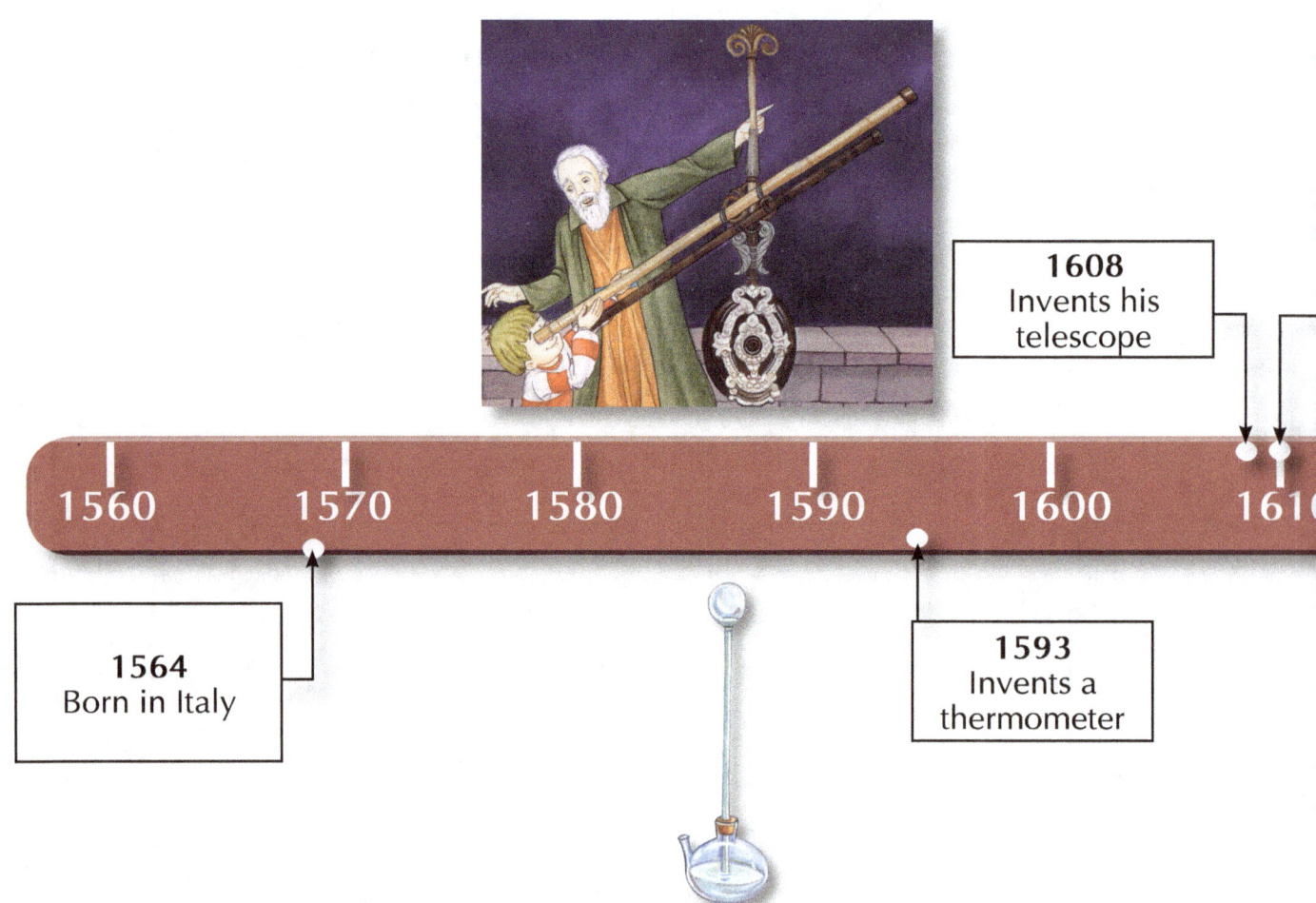

1608
Invents his
telescope

1560   1570   1580   1590   1600   1610

1564
Born in Italy

1593
Invents a
thermometer

Galileo Galilei's Life and Work

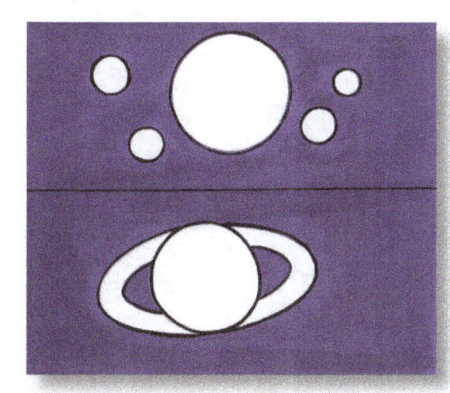

1610
Discovers four
moons moving
around Jupiter

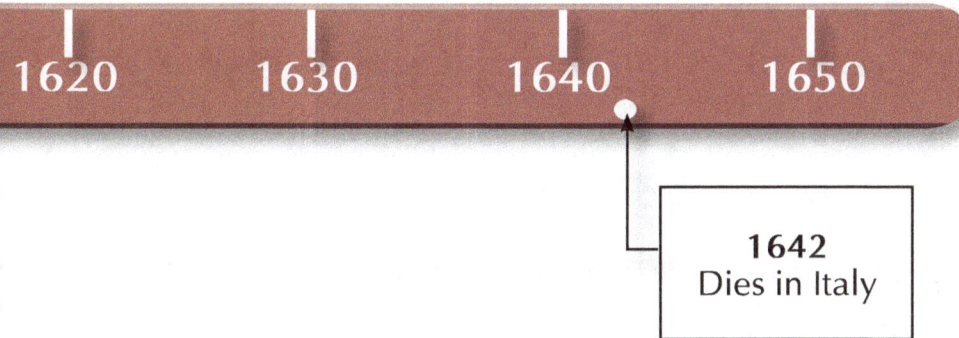

1620   1630   1640   1650

1642
Dies in Italy

Word Meanings

Astronomer: A scientist who studies outer space

Experiments: Tests to discover something new

Galaxy: A very large group of stars held together in the universe

Inventor: Someone who designs or creates something that did not exist before

Italy: A country in Europe

Jupiter: The biggest planet in our solar system. It is fifth from the Sun, after Mars and before Saturn

Milky Way: The galaxy that includes the Earth, seen at night as a pale strip across the sky

Planets: Large bodies that move around a star

Saturn: The second biggest planet in our solar system. Saturn has rings made of ice, dust and rocks

Solar System: The sun and the group of planets that move around it

Telescope: A tubular instrument for viewing distant objects in outer space

Thermometer: A tool that measures temperature

Think, Talk and Write

Think About It

Galileo Galilei liked to learn new things.
Think about what you just read.
List three things he liked to study.

Talk About It

Talk with your family and friends about Galileo's work.
Then ask a family member to look at the night sky with you.
Talk about what you see. Later draw what you saw.

Write About It

Galileo solved problems with his inventions.
What could you invent?
Make a drawing of your invention.
Write three sentences. Tell what problem it solves.

What did you learn from Galileo Galilei?

....

....

....

....

....

....

....

....

....

....

....

....

....

....

What are the five things that you will change after reading Galileo Galilei's story?

....
....
....
....
....
....
....
....
....
....
....
....
....
....
....

Albert Einstein

Albert Einstein was a great thinker.
His ideas were so different that few people understood them.
What was so special about his ideas?
Read on to discover the answer.

Meet Tim and Tyra

Hi, I'm Tim.

Hi, I'm Tyra. We are going to travel back in time to visit Albert Einstein. Let's meet him now.

Hello, Tim. Hello, Tyra. Welcome to my house. I'd like to tell you about my life and show you some of the things I've done.

Hi, Mr Einstein.

Hello, Mr Einstein.

Albert Einstein was born in Ulm, **Germany** on 14 March, 1879.
He was a great scientist.

Albert Einstein did not like school.
He liked to study all by himself.
He loved to think about things.
He was always curious.

One day, his father gave him a **magnetic compass**.
He saw that the needle always pointed north. He wondered why?
Einstein was only five.

Albert Einstein could not find any work in Germany.
So he moved to **Switzerland**.
He got a job at the **patent** office in **Bern**.
He worked as a patent **clerk**.

The job was boring.
But it gave him a lot of time to study physics.
He wrote his famous **theories** while working in Bern.

Albert Einstein had a great mind.
He imagined many things that few people thought possible.
He wrote down his imaginations as theories.
His ideas came to be known as the "Special Theory of Relativity."
The year was 1905.

Albert Einstein wrote an **equation**.
The equation was $E = mc^2$.
The equation made him very famous.

For the next ten years, Albert Einstein worked on a new theory.
In 1915, he completed his theory.
He called his theory "General Theory of Relativity."

Einstein said that light did not always travel in a straight line.
He said that light could bend because of **gravity**.
This was a new idea then.

In 1919, his theory was proved right.
Einstein became famous all over the world.

Albert Einstein won a big prize in 1921.
It was the **Nobel Prize**.

Albert Einstein moved to the USA in 1933. He became an American citizen.
He worked as a professor in **Princeton**, USA.
He lived there for the rest of his life.

Albert Einstein was a great scientist.
He loved thinking and learning all his life.

He died in Princeton, USA on 18 April, 1955.

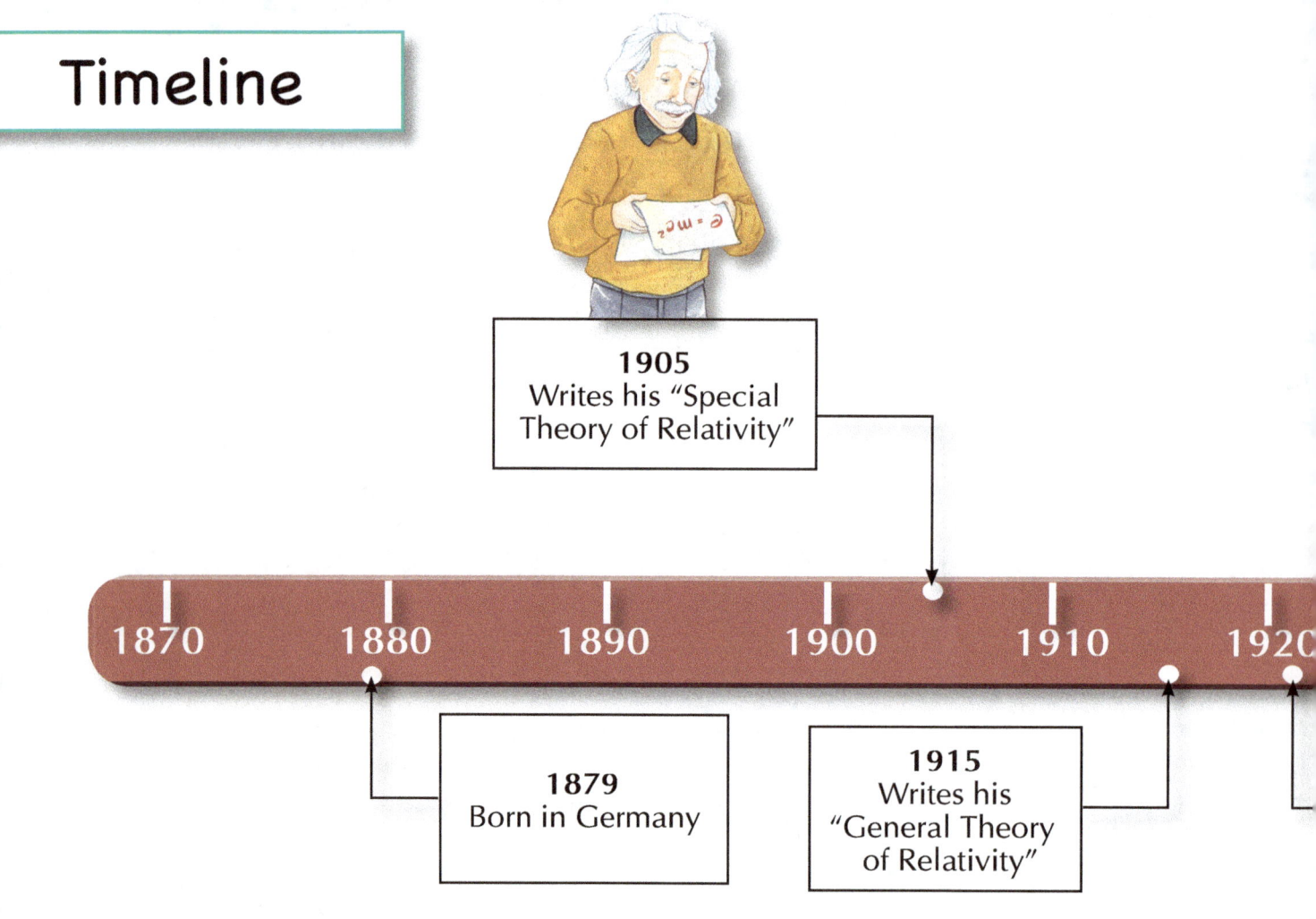

1905
Writes his "Special
Theory of Relativity"

1879
Born in Germany

1915
Writes his
"General Theory
of Relativity"

1870   1880   1890   1900   1910   1920

Albert Einstein's Life and Work

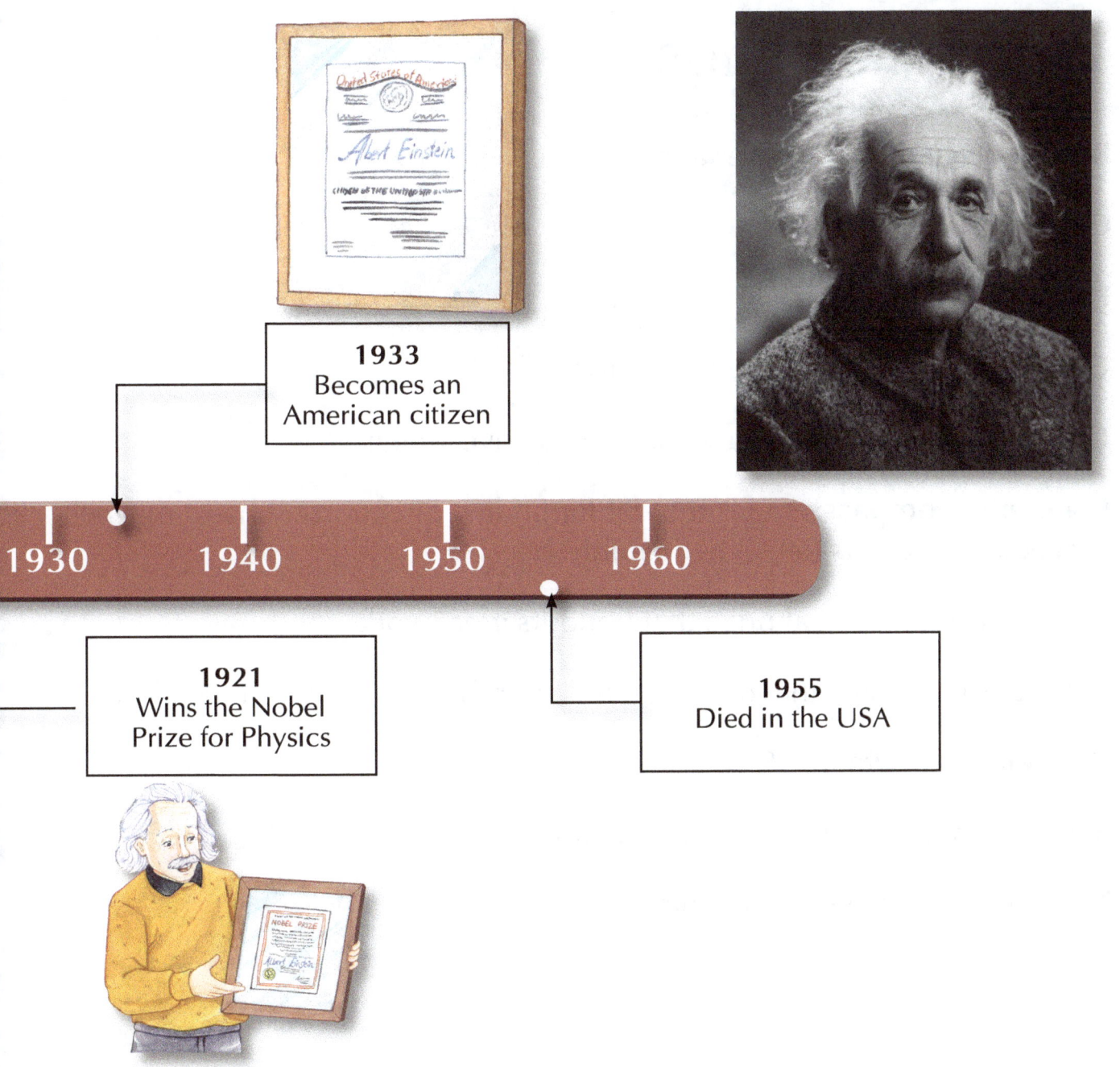

1933
Becomes an
American citizen

1930   1940   1950   1960

1921
Wins the Nobel
Prize for Physics

1955
Died in the USA

Word Meanings

Bern: The capital of Switzerland

Clerk: An office worker

Equation: A mathematical sentence

Germany: A country in western Europe

Gravity: The force that causes objects to have weight

Magnetic Compass: An instrument for finding directions. It has a magnetic needle that points to magnetic north

Nobel Prize: A special prize that honours great work

Patent: A document that makes an inventor the owner of his invention

Princeton: A town in USA

Switzerland: A country in central Europe

Theory: A set of ideas that explains something

Think, Talk and Write

Think About It

How did Albert Einstein's early years help him become a scientist? Write a list of things that helped Albert Einstein become a scientist.

Talk About It

What interests you most about Einstein?
Tell a classmate about Einstein.
Explain to a classmate what interests you most about Einstein.

Write About It

Would you like to be a scientist?
Write about why you would or would not like to be a scientist.

What did you learn from Albert Einstein?

....

....

....

....

....

....

....

....

....

....

....

....

....

....

What are the five things that you will change after reading Albert Einstein's story?

....
....
....
....
....
....
....
....
....
....
....
....
....
....

Isaac Newton

Isaac Newton made many important discoveries.
What were these discoveries?
Why were they so important?
Read on to discover the answer.

Meet Tim and Tyra

Hi, I'm Tim.

Hi, I'm Tyra. We are going to travel back in time to visit Isaac Newton. Let's meet him now.

88

Isaac Newton was born in Lincolnshire, England on 25 December, 1642. He was a great scientist and inventor.

Chapter 2: The Apple

Isaac Newton loved to think and **experiment**.

One day, he saw an apple fall from a tree.

He wondered what made the apple to fall to the ground.

He did some experiments.

He found that a force pulled the apple to the ground.

He called this force 'gravity.'

Isaac Newton did many experiments with light.
He passed sunlight through a prism.
He found that sunlight broke up into different colours.
He made a note of the **spectrum** of colours.
He recognized the seven colours of the spectrum as
red, orange, yellow, green, blue, indigo and violet.

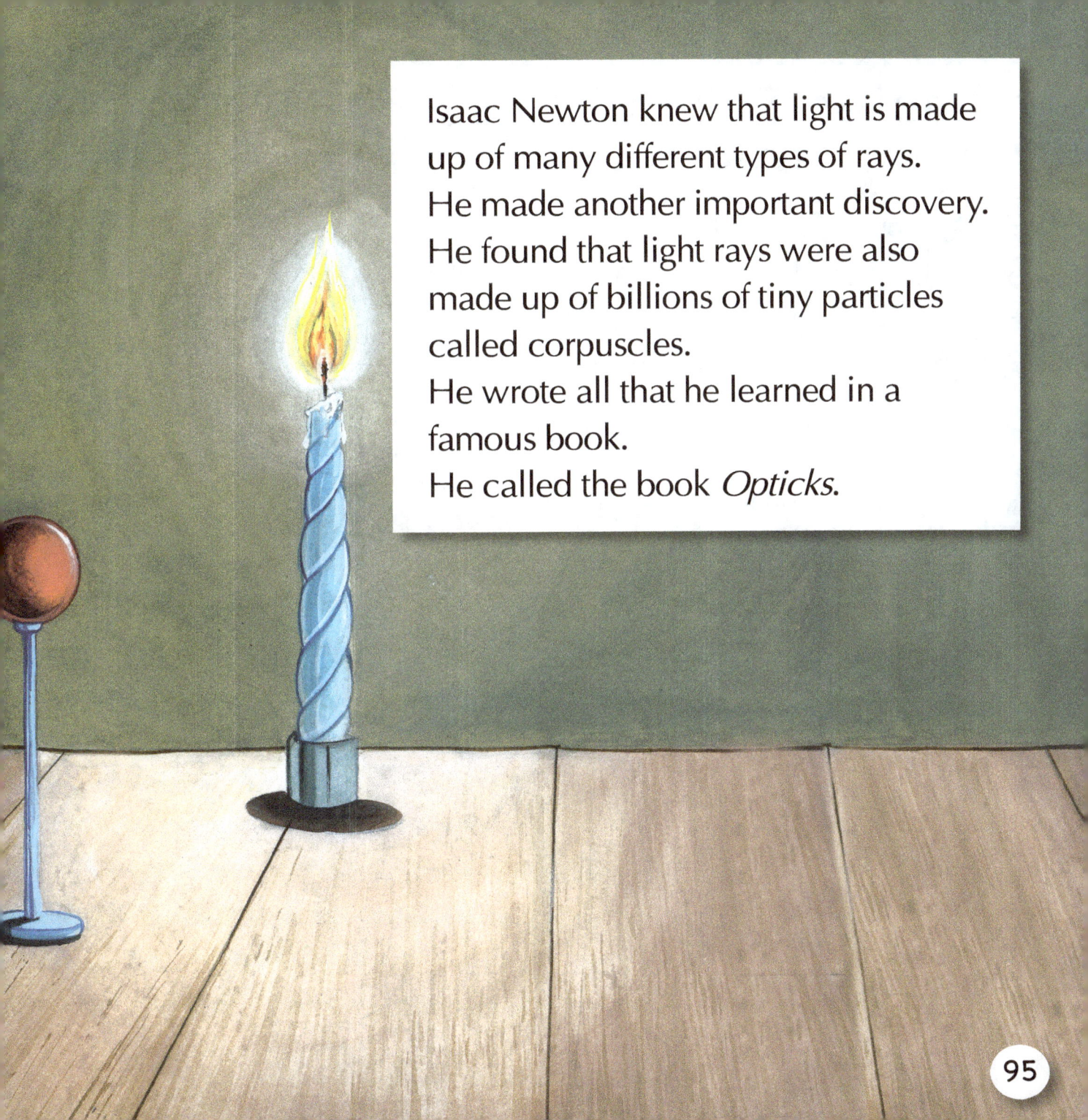

Isaac Newton knew that light is made up of many different types of rays.
He made another important discovery.
He found that light rays were also made up of billions of tiny particles called corpuscles.
He wrote all that he learned in a famous book.
He called the book *Opticks*.

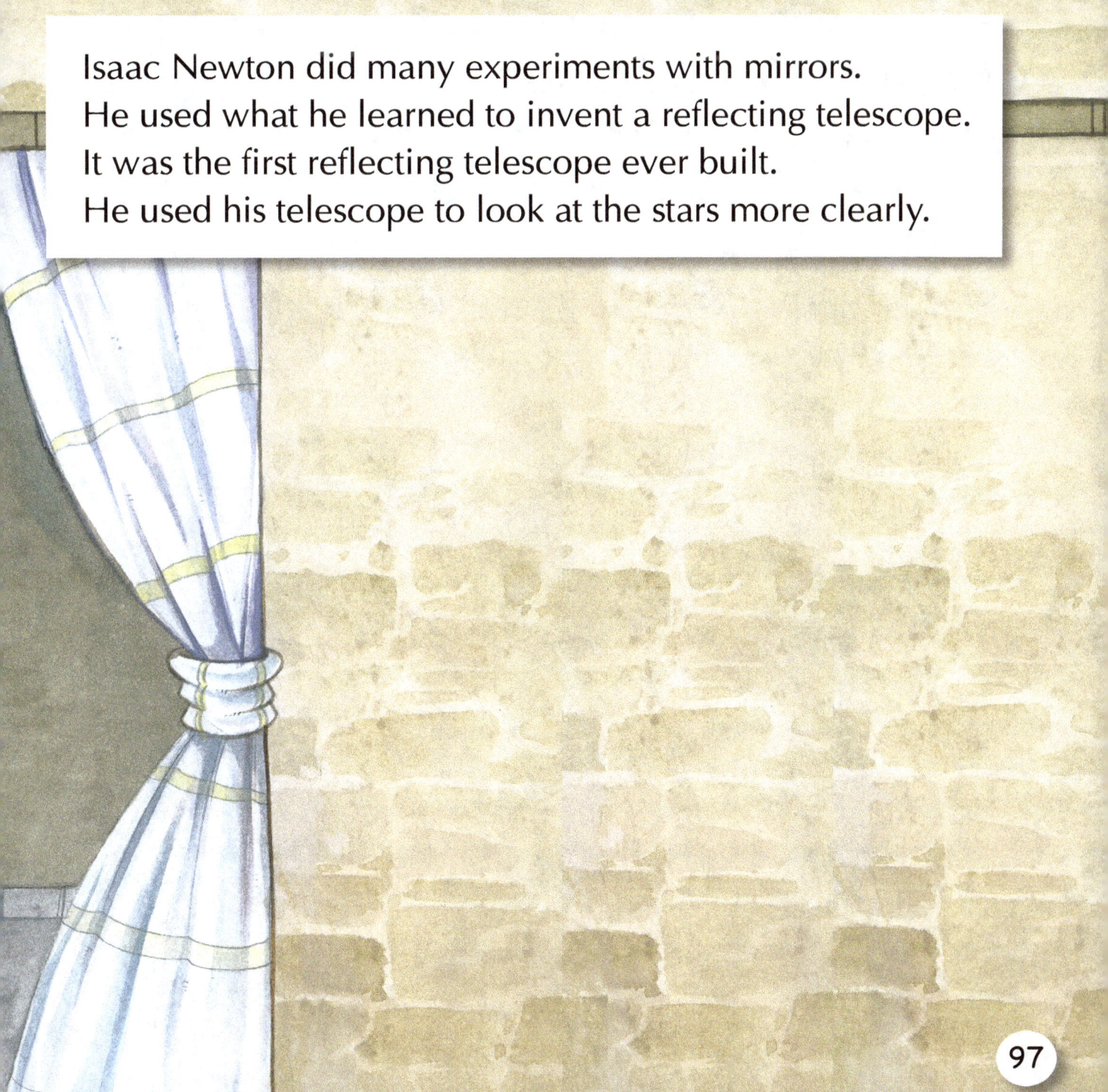

Isaac Newton did many experiments with mirrors.
He used what he learned to invent a reflecting telescope.
It was the first reflecting telescope ever built.
He used his telescope to look at the stars more clearly.

Isaac Newton believed the math of his time was not enough to solve all problems of science. What could he do?

He **invented** a new type of math. It is called calculus. Calculus helped him solve many difficult problems.

Isaac Newton wrote a famous book.
He called it *Philosophiae Naturalis Principia Mathematica*.
It means "Mathematical Principles of Natural Philosophy."
It was written in **Latin**.
The book contains his famous laws of motion and gravitation.

The book made him a well-known scientist.
He was made the President of the **Royal Society**.

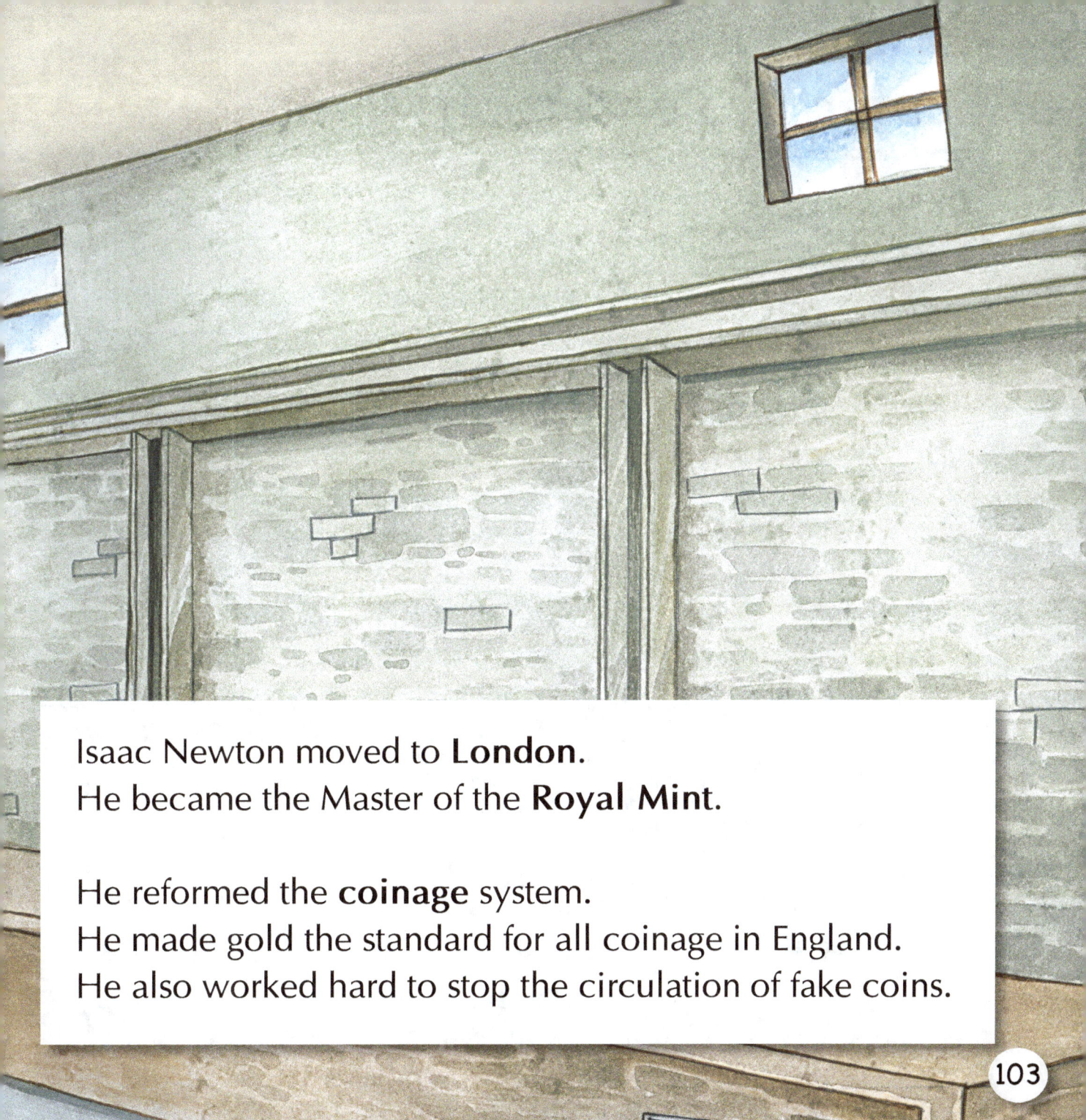

Isaac Newton moved to **London**.
He became the Master of the **Royal Mint**.

He reformed the **coinage** system.
He made gold the standard for all coinage in England.
He also worked hard to stop the circulation of fake coins.

Isaac Newton was a great scientist and thinker.
He was the first scientist to be made a **Knight** by the
Queen of England. It was a great honour for a great man.

Newton died in London, England on 20 March, 1726.

Timeline

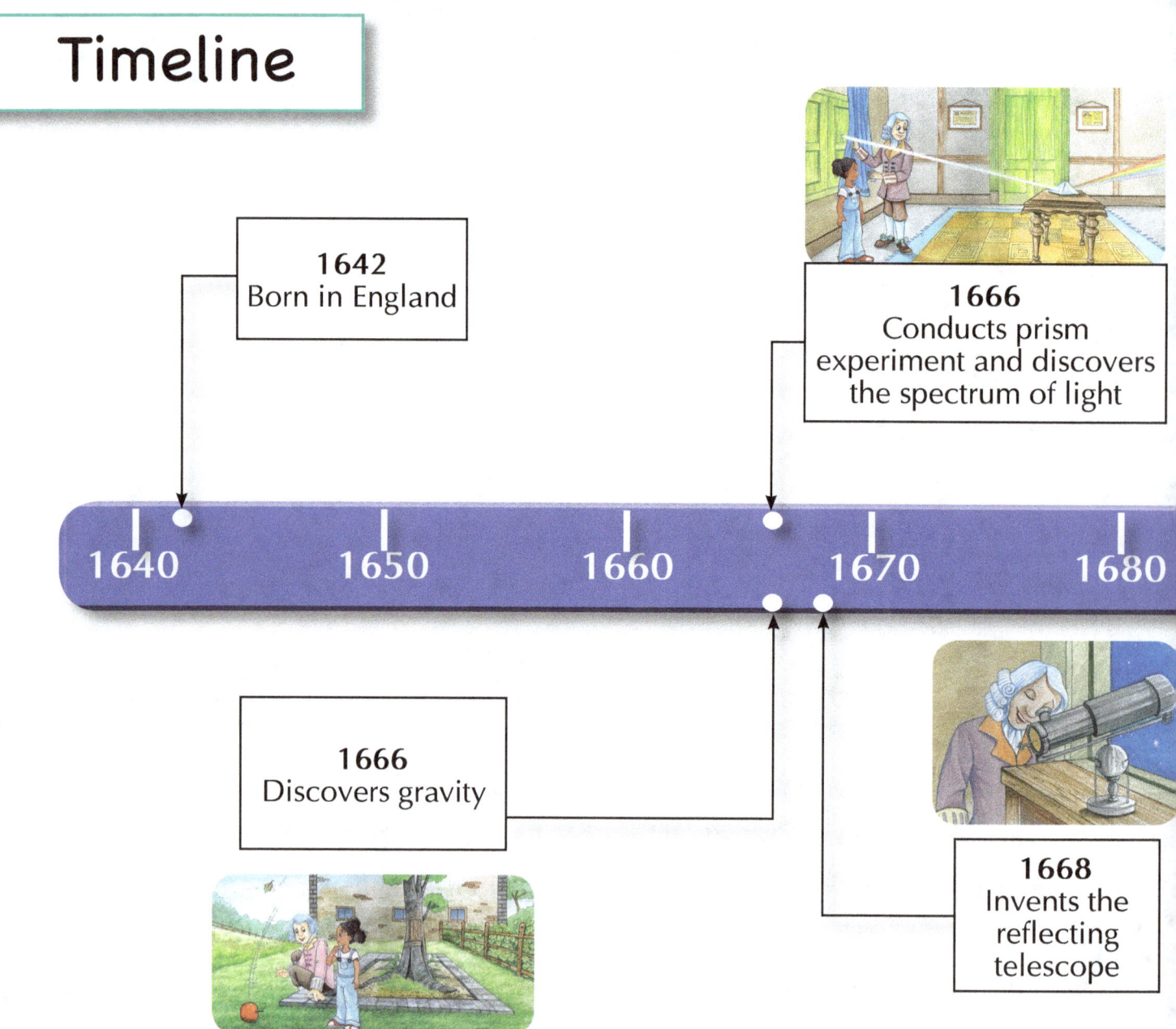

1642
Born in England

1666
Conducts prism experiment and discovers the spectrum of light

1666
Discovers gravity

1640   1650   1660   1670   1680

1668
Invents the reflecting telescope

Isaac Newton's Life and Work

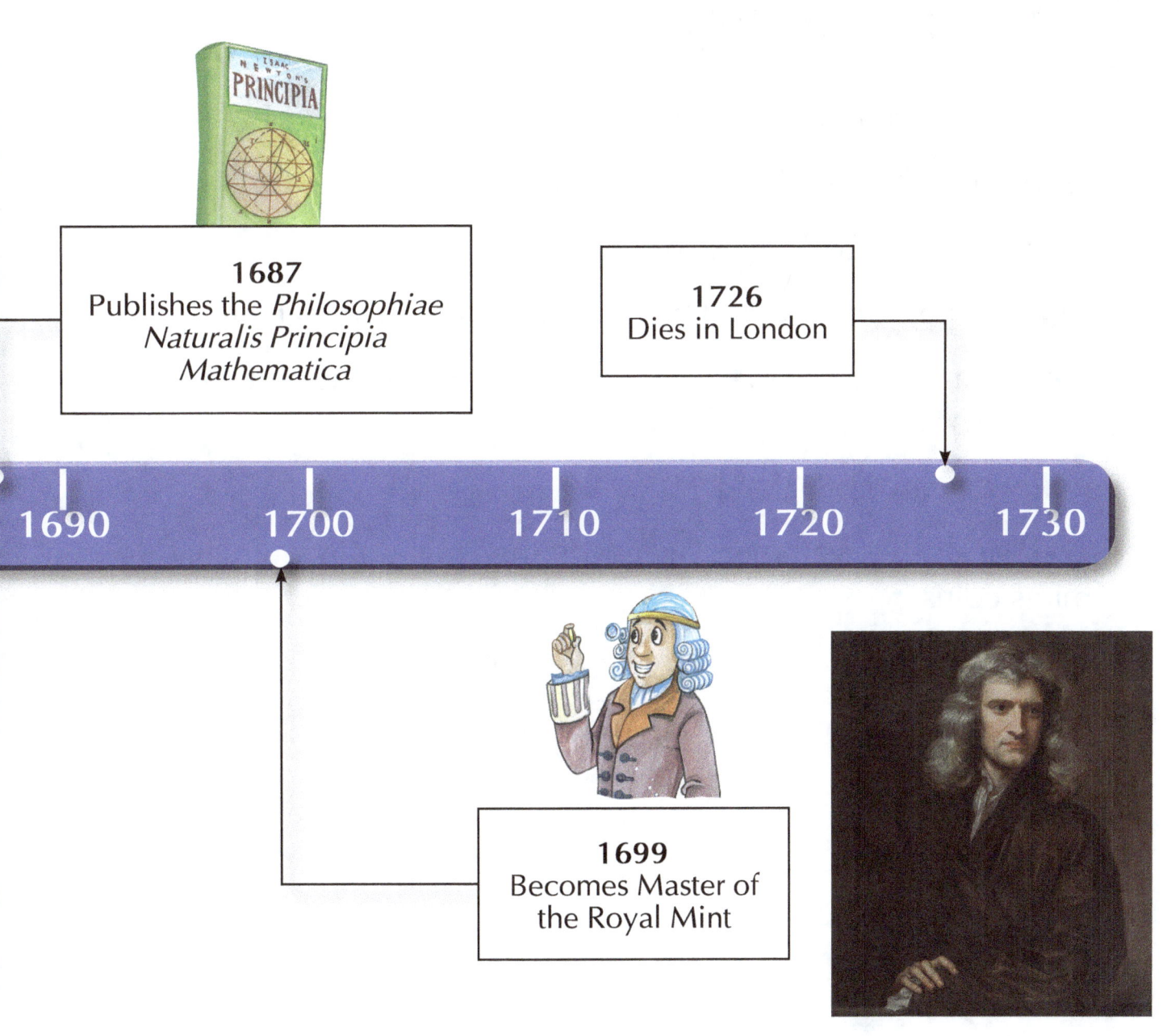

1687
Publishes the *Philosophiae Naturalis Principia Mathematica*

1726
Dies in London

1690   1700   1710   1720   1730

1699
Becomes Master of the Royal Mint

Word Meanings

Coinage: Coins circulated as money

Experiment: Test to discover something new

Invented: Made something for the first time

Knight: A person honoured by the Queen for personal merit

Latin: A language originally spoken in Ancient Rome and widely used by scientists

London: A city in England

Royal Mint: A government agency in the United Kingdom that mints coins

Royal Society: A famous society of scientists

Spectrum: A multicoloured band of light

Think, Talk and Write

Think About It

Isaac Newton liked to learn new things.
Think about what you just read.
List three things he liked to study.

Talk About It

Talk with your family and friends about Newton's discoveries.
Share what you know with your friends or family.
Tell them why you think his discoveries were important.
Ask what they know about Newton.

Write About It

Newton solved many problems with his inventions.
What could you invent?
Make a drawing of your invention.
Write three sentences. Tell what problem it solves.

What did you learn from Isaac Newton?

....

....

....

....

....

....

....

....

....

....

....

....

....

....

What are the five things that you will change after reading Isaac Newton's story?

....
....
....
....
....
....
....
....
....
....
....
....
....
....

Work Space

www.ingramcontent.com/pod-product-compliance
Lightning Source LLC
Chambersburg PA
CBHW080959020726
47505CB00009B/2257